D1134227

A TEMPLAR BOOK

Produced by The Templar Company plc,
Pippbrook Mill, London Road, Dorking, Surrey RH4 1JE, Great Britain.

This edition produced for Parragon Books,
Unit 13-17, Avonbridge Trading Estate, Atlantic Road, Avonmouth, Bristol BS11 9Q

This book contains material first published as
Very Young the Wizard in Enid Blyton's Sunny Stories
and Sunny Stories between 1926 and 1953.

Illustrated by Alison Winfield

Printed and bound in Italy

ISBN 1 85813 553 2

POCKET LIBRARY

WHISKERS AND THE WIZARD

Illustrated by Alison Winfield

PARRAGON

There was once a wizard called Blunder. He was the youngest and smallest of all the wizards, and he was not very good at learning magic.

He made so many mistakes that all the other wizards laughed at him.

"One of these days you'll cast a magic spell on yourself by mistake," they said, "and then you'll be in a fine pickle!"

But Blunder wouldn't listen to any advice. He thought he knew everything.

He carried on making spells, stirring up strange recipes for magic in his boiling cauldron, and muttering enchanted words to himself. He had one servant – a faithful little rabbit called Whiskers. Most wizards, like witches, have cats for servants, for cats are wise and can keep secrets. But magic cats cost a great deal of money and Blunder couldn't afford one. So he had a rabbit instead, which was much cheaper.

Whiskers was a very clean and tidy servant. He swept and dusted, cooked and mended and looked after Blunder very well indeed. Sometimes he stirred the cauldron himself, though he was afraid of what magic might come out of it.

When he saw that Blunder often made mistakes, he was worried in case the little wizard should harm himself. He was very fond of his master, and wouldn't have let anything happen to him for all the world. So one day Whiskers asked if he could look at all the magic books. That way he thought he might learn some magic himself, and perhaps be able to help Blunder one day. But Blunder just laughed at him.

"Why, you're only a rabbit!" he said. "You'll

never be able to learn any magic. But you can
look at my magic books if you like."

So Whiskers waited until his work was done.
Then he took down the magic books one by one,
and read them all. He had a good memory, and
very soon he knew a great many spells, and could
say hundreds of magic words.

One day he saw Blunder mixing spiders' webs,
blue mushrooms and the yolk from a goose's egg,
chanting as he went,

> "Tick-a-too, fa-la-lee,
> Ta-ra, ta-ra, ta-roo,
> Dickety, hickety, jiminy-japes,
> Bibble and scribble and boo!"

"Master! Master!" cried Whiskers,
dropping his broom in a hurry.
"You're saying the wrong words!
Instead of making magic to grow
a goose that lays golden eggs,
you are saying a spell that
will turn you into a
goose yourself!"

It was true! Blunder had made a mistake. Already feathers had begun to sprout from his shoulders! Hurriedly he began to chant the right spell, and the feathers slowly disappeared.

But instead of being grateful to Whiskers, he was cross with him!

"I'd soon have found out my mistake!" he said sharply. "Get on with your work, Whiskers, and in future don't interfere in things that you know nothing about."

The next day, the powerful Wizard of Woz came to tea, but he arrived with bad news.

"The wicked goblin has been seen again in Pixie Wood," said the old wizard. "So we want *you* to get rid of him, Blunder. Or better still, make

some magic that will get him into our power. Then we can make him into a useful servant. You know how to do it, don't you?"

"Of course I do!" said Blunder.

"You can trust me to do a simple thing like that! The goblin will be in your power before midnight."

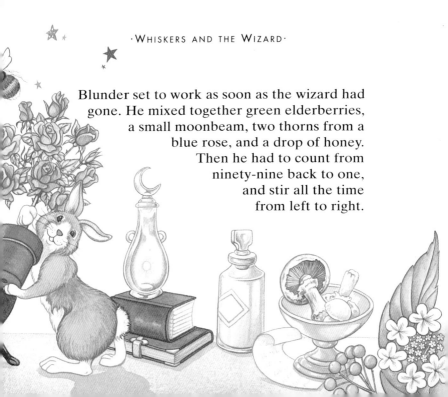

Blunder set to work as soon as the wizard had gone. He mixed together green elderberries, a small moonbeam, two thorns from a blue rose, and a drop of honey. Then he had to count from ninety-nine back to one, and stir all the time from left to right.

"Ninety-nine, ninety-eight, ninety-seven," began Blunder and he had almost got to twenty, when Whiskers gave a cry of fear.

"Master! You're stirring the wrong way! Oh dear, oh dear, you'll put yourself in the goblin's power, instead of getting him into yours!"

Blunder stopped stirring in fright and began stirring the other way – but you can't do that sort of thing in the middle of a powerful spell! Something is bound to happen, and all of a sudden it did! There was a tremendous BANG and a blue-green flame shot out of the cauldron and whizzed twice around the room. Then it turned into a swirling purple wind that whisked Blunder up into the air and out of the window!

Whiskers crouched in a corner and waited for something else to happen. But nothing did – except that he heard a very strange laugh from somewhere that made him shiver and tremble.

"That was the goblin!" thought the little rabbit. "He knows that Blunder has put himself in his power, and he's come to get him. Oh dear, I must try to rescue him at once!"

Meanwhile Blunder had flown out of the window, risen as high as the clouds, and then come down, bump, in a place he didn't know!

"This is a fine thing!" he said. "Now what am I to do?" But at that moment he heard a horrid laugh, and suddenly there in front of him stood the wicked little goblin.

"Ho ho!" said the goblin. "Now you're in *my* power, Blunder. You don't deserve to be a wizard when you make such silly mistakes. Come along, I'm going to keep you in my cave and you can be my servant!"

"Never!" cried Blunder. "I won't go."

But the goblin knew a little magic too. He muttered a few strange words, and at once Blunder's feet began to walk in the direction that the goblin wished them to.

"You will stay here until I get back," said the wicked goblin when they had reached his cave. "And just in case you try to misbehave, this will stop you."

He drew a white chalk circle right around poor Blunder who watched him in dismay, for he knew that the circle was a magic one and would stop him using any spells to escape.

"Please set me free," Blunder begged.

But the goblin would not listen. He just clapped his hands seven times, laughed and disappeared. At the same time a great stone rolled over the entrance to the cave, leaving Blunder all alone in the cold and dark.

"No one but Whiskers knows I am gone!" he wept. "And how will he be able to help me? He's only a silly little rabbit."

Little did Blunder know at that very moment Whiskers was busy searching for him. He had just reached the edge of Goblin Land and was trying to decide which way to go first.

"Now what I need is that spell I read the other day," muttered Whiskers to himself. "That will help me find my master."

Soon he had remembered what to do. He took five green leaves and put them in a circle with their ends touching. Then he found a white feather and blew it into the air, singing the magic words as he did so. When he looked down again, the leaves had vanished! But the feather was still floating in front of him, floating away to the west as if blown by a strong breeze.

"Lead me to my master!"
cried the rabbit, and followed
the feather as it danced off
down the hillside.

Soon it brought Whiskers to
the cave. As soon as the little
rabbit saw the great stone at the
entrance he felt certain that his
master was imprisoned behind it.

"Master, Master!" he called out. "Are you there? It's me, Whiskers." Inside the cave, Blunder could not believe his ears.

"Oh, Whiskers, is it really you!" he cried. "I have been trapped in here by the wicked goblin. Can you help me escape? Can you move the stone?"

But even though Whiskers pushed against the great stone with all his strength; he could not move it even one inch.

"Never mind," said the little wizard, in despair. "Even if you could move it, it wouldn't be much use, for I can't move out of this magic circle. And even if I knew how to do that, I can't remember the spell that would get rid of the goblin's power."

"Perhaps I can help," cried the little rabbit.
"I think I can remember the spell about goblins."
And he started to recite it carefully to Blunder.

"That's just the one I want!" cried Blunder.
"Oh, Whiskers! If only you could gather all the
ingredients together, I might be able to escape.
But I'm afraid it's quite impossible."

"Why's that?" said Whiskers in dismay.

"Because the final ingredient is a hair from my
head," explained Blunder. "So unless we can move
this stone, I'm stuck. I shall have to be that horrid
goblin's slave forever."

Whiskers pushed at the great stone again, but it
was no use. Then he had a brilliant idea! Wasn't he
a rabbit? Couldn't he burrow like all rabbits do?

At once he began to burrow
into the hillside, just beside the
cave entrance. He sent out the
earth in great showers, and
in minutes he had made a
tunnel into the cave
where Blunder sat.

"Hurray!" cried Blunder. "You're quite the most brilliant rabbit in the whole world. Now we can get to work."

The little wizard knew that the one thing that could destroy the goblin's power was the sight of a red, frilled dragon. And the spell told them exactly how to make one. So all that day and all that night brave little Whiskers went in and out of his tunnel, fetching nightshade berries, white feathers, blue toadstools, sunbeams, moonbeams and everything else that Blunder needed.

Soon all the ingredients were neatly piled at one end of the enormous cave. Whiskers put the last one on the very top and then sat down with his master to wait for the goblin to return.

Early the next morning they heard the goblin outside the cave. He shouted a magic word, and the stone flew away from the entrance. Then he strode in. Whiskers had hidden himself, and Blunder was pretending to be asleep.

"Ho ho! Ha ha!" said the goblin. "What about a nice hot breakfast, Blunder? You must be hungry by now."

The wizard pretended to groan.

"Well, tell me a few secret spells and I will give you some toast and eggs," said the goblin.

"Here is one," said Blunder, raising his head, and he began to chant the spell that would turn

all the magic things at the end of the cave into a
fearful frilled dragon! The goblin listened carefully,
grinning all the while because he thought that he
was hearing a wonderful new spell.

Then, just as Blunder got to the last words, a
strange thing happened. A rushing, swishing noise
came from the end of the cave, and suddenly a
dreadful bellow rang out. Then two yellow eyes
gleamed, and lo and behold! A great dragon
came rushing out!

"A frilled dragon!" yelled the goblin in fright.
"Oh my! Oh my! A great, red frilled dragon! Let
me out! Let me go!"

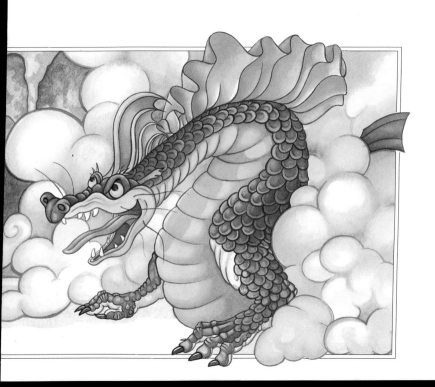

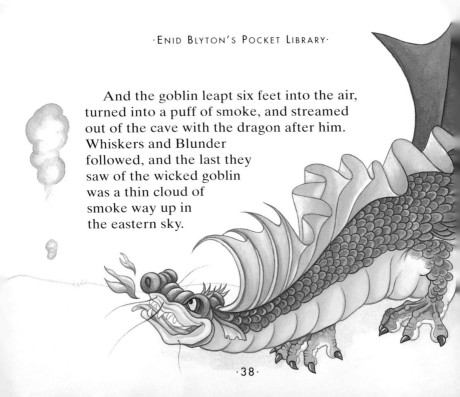

And the goblin leapt six feet into the air, turned into a puff of smoke, and streamed out of the cave with the dragon after him. Whiskers and Blunder followed, and the last they saw of the wicked goblin was a thin cloud of smoke way up in the eastern sky.

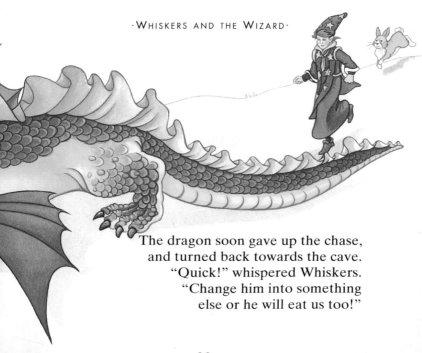

The dragon soon gave up the chase,
and turned back towards the cave.
"Quick!" whispered Whiskers.
"Change him into something
else or he will eat us too!"

Blunder clapped his hands twice, and uttered a command. The dragon began to shrink, and when it was as small as a football it turned into a mass of red flames.

Whiskers hurriedly filled a jug with water and gave it to Blunder, who threw it over the flames – and sizzle-sizzle-sizzle, they went out! Nothing was left of the frilled dragon except for a few wet ashes.

"My goodness," said Blunder, sitting down on the ground with a sigh. "We have been having too many adventures, Whiskers. I shall be glad to get home, and sleep in my soft bed!"

"Poor Master, you must be very tired," said the kind rabbit. "Jump up on my back, and I'll take you home before you can say 'Tiddley-winks'!"

So Blunder climbed up on Whiskers' soft back, and very soon he was safely home.

"Thank you very much for all you have done for me," said the little wizard, hugging the delighted rabbit. "I think you are much cleverer than I am, Whiskers."

"From now on you shall be my partner, not my servant, and you shall wear a pointed hat like me! We will do all our spells together, and then perhaps I shan't ever make a mistake again!"

Whiskers was so pleased.

"Well, let's go to bed now and have some sleep," said Blunder, yawning. "I can hardly keep my eyes open. Then tomorrow, we will go and buy your pointed hat." So they both fell asleep, and Whiskers dreamed happily of wearing a pointed hat and helping Blunder with his spells.

Many years have passed since Blunder has his adventure with the wicked goblin. Whiskers is still with him, but now Blunder is very old, and Whiskers' ears have gone grey with age.

Sometimes when all their work is done, they sit one on each side of the fireplace, and Whiskers says: "Do you remember that time when you made a mistake in your spells?"

Then they both laugh loudly, and wonder where the wicked goblin went to – for he has never been heard of from that day to this.